A NOTE TO PARENTS

Disney's First Readers Level 2 books were created for beginning readers who are gaining confidence in their early reading skills.

Compared to Level 1 books, **Level 2** books have slightly smaller type and contain more words to a page. Although sentence structure is still simple, the stories are slightly longer and more complex.

Just as children need training wheels when learning to ride a bicycle, they need the support of a good model when learning to read. Every time your child sees that you enjoy reading, whether alone or with him or her, you provide the encouragement needed to build reading confidence. Here are some helpful hints to use with the **Disney's First Readers Level 2** books:

★ Play or act out each character's words. Change your voice to indicate which character is speaking. As your child becomes comfortable with the printed text, he or she can take a favorite character's part and read those passages.

★ Have your child try reading the story. If your child asks about a word, do not interrupt the flow of reading to make him or her sound it out. Pronounce the word for your child. If, however, he or she begins to sound it out, be gently encouraging—your child is developing phonetic skills!

★ Read aloud. It's still important at this level to read to your child. With your child watching, move a finger smoothly along the text. Do not stop at each word. Change the tone of your voice to indicate punctuation marks, such as questions and exclamations. Your child will begin to notice how print makes sense and makes reading fun.

★ Let your child ask you questions about the story. This helps to develop your child's critical thinking skills. Use the After-Reading Fun activities provided at the end of each book as a fun exercise to further enhance your child's reading skills.

★ Praise all reading efforts warmly and often!

Remember that early-reading experiences that you share with your child can help your child to become a confident and successful reader later on!

— Patricia Koppman
Past President
International Reading Association

DISNEP'S

Winnie the Pooh

Pooh's Wake-up Song

by Isabel Gaines
Illustrated by Josie Yee

Disney's First Readers — Level 2

SCHOLASTIC INC.

New York   Toronto   London   Auckland   Sydney
Mexico City   New Delhi   Hong Kong   Buenos Aires

The sun streamed in
through Pooh's window.
"What a happy day!" he said.

Pooh got out of bed.

He stretched up.

He stretched down.

Then he ate
a big jar of honey.

It was nice outside,
so Pooh decided to take a walk.

While Pooh walked,
he made up a song.
"I had some honey.
Today is so sunny.
Hum, dee, ho, hummy."

Soon Pooh came
to Rabbit's house.
"Hum, dee, dee,
dum, dum," Pooh sang.

Rabbit poked his head
out of his window.
"Pooh, you woke
me up!" said Rabbit.

"I'm sorry," said Pooh.
"Would you like to sing with me?"

"No," said Rabbit.

Rabbit slammed his window shut
and went back to bed.
Pooh continued his walk.

The next day was also
bright and sunny.
Pooh woke up
in a happy mood.

Pooh got out of bed.

He stretched up.

He stretched down.

Then he ate
a big jar of honey.

Once again,
he went out for a walk.
"The sun is so sunny,
I want more honey," sang Pooh.

When Pooh walked by
Rabbit's house,
Pooh saw something new.

"Rabbit has a sign,
and it looks so fine,"
Pooh sang.

"Pooh, you woke me up again!"
shouted a sleepy Rabbit.

"Sorry, Rabbit," said Pooh.
"I like your new sign."

NO SINGING IN THE MORNING

"Thank you," said Rabbit.
"I made it. It says,
No Singing in the Morning!"

"You did a very nice job,"
said Pooh.

The next morning,
Pooh decided to walk
in the other direction.

Rabbit slept happily
in his bed until he heard,
"Chirp, chirpety, chirp."
"Is that you, Pooh?" Rabbit called.

He looked out his window,
but Pooh was nowhere in sight.
Then Rabbit saw
a bird's nest on the sign.

"Chirp, chirpety, chirp,"
sang the baby birds
in the nest.

"Oh dear," said Rabbit.

He couldn't tell the baby birds
to be quiet.
They were so cute.
Their song was so sweet.

The next morning,
Rabbit awoke once again
to the baby birds singing.

He tried to be mad at them.
But as he listened to their song,
Rabbit discovered he rather liked it.

Then Rabbit heard Pooh
coming down the path.
Pooh was singing, too.
And his song matched
the baby birds' song.

Rabbit had an idea.
He jumped out of bed
and ran outside.

When Pooh arrived
at Rabbit's house,
he noticed Rabbit's sign
was different.

PLEASE
NO SINGING
IN THE
MORNING

"What happened to your sign?"
asked Pooh.

"I fixed it," said Rabbit.
"Now it says,
Please Sing in the Morning."

"What a wonderful idea!"
said Pooh.

"Would you like to join me in a song or two now?" Pooh asked.

"I most certainly would," said Rabbit.

And from that day on,
Pooh and Rabbit started every day
with a song.

AFTER-READING FUN

Enhance the reading experience with follow-up questions to help your child develop reading comprehension and increase his/her awareness of words.

Approach this with a sense of play. Make a game of having your child answer the questions. You do not need to ask all the questions at one time. Let these questions be fun discussions rather than a test. If your child doesn't have instant recall, encourage him/her to look back into the book to "research" the answers. You'll be modeling what good readers do and, at the same time, forging a sharing bond with your child.

1. What did Pooh do each morning when he woke up?

2. Why did Pooh take a walk in the morning?

3. Why didn't Rabbit like Pooh's singing?

4. What did Rabbit do to stop Pooh's singing?

5. Why did Rabbit change the sign to say: Please sing in the morning?

6. What song do you like to sing most of all?